Kobee Manatee

Heading Home to Florida

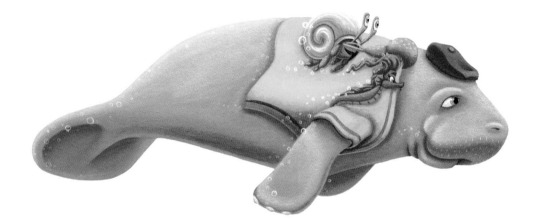

Written By **Robert Scott Thayer**

Illustrated By **Lauren Gallegos**

Thompson Mill Press

To Mom ... this one's for you.
-R.S.T.

For my friend, Kirsti, who loves all the sea creatures.
-L.G.

Text copyright © 2013 by Robert Scott Thayer
Illustrations © 2013 by Lauren Gallegos

Many thanks go out to all who helped in the making of this book, in particular; Susan Korman, Susan Heyboer O'Keefe, Eileen Robinson, Kathy Temean and Dr. Katie Tripp (Save the Manatee Club).

Published by Thompson Mill Press LLC
www.thompsonmillpress.com

Library of Congress Cataloging in Publication Data
Thayer, Robert Scott.
Kobee manatee: heading home to Florida / written by Robert Scott Thayer; illustrated by Lauren Gallegos. – 1st ed.
p. cm.
Summary: Kobee Manatee enjoys a rare summertime trip from Florida all the way up to Cape Cod, Massachusetts, but needs to get back home before winter, as he encounters several obstacles and two new friends along the way.

ISBN 978-0-9883269-2-7 (hardcover)   2012954847

Printed and Bound in the USA

The illustrations were created with acrylic on illustration board.
First edition, second printing November 2016
Designed by Lauren Gallegos.

I'm Kobee Manatee. I swam from Florida to Cape Cod, Massachusetts. Manatees rarely travel this far, but I love adventures.

It's chilly in Cape Cod Bay this September day. So I'm heading home to Blue Spring State Park in Florida before winter, or I'll die from the cold.

Kobee's Fun Facts

Hi, I'm Kobee. I'm a West Indian manatee, also called a Florida manatee. You'll find me in Florida's waters during winter. I'm warm blooded and need water temperatures around seventy degrees Fahrenheit. During summer, I'll travel the Gulf of Mexico, or the southeast coast of the United States.

I rolled upside down for good luck, then swam out to the Atlantic Ocean for my twelve hundred mile journey south.

Kobee's Fun Facts

Most manatees stay in Florida all year. Only a small percentage (less than 10%) leave Florida in the warm months.

Manatees like traveling at three to five miles per hour. On an adventure, they can travel at speeds up to twenty miles per hour on short bursts!

Soon I met a seahorse named Tess. She was lost and wanted warmer water. "I'm going to Florida where there's lots of warm water, hop on," I said.

"What's your name?" she asked.

"Kobee," I said.

"You look like a BIG submarine! What are you?" she asked.

I laughed and said, "A manatee."

"A manatee in New England, that's cool!" replied Tess.

I chuckled, "It's too cool, so we're heading to warm Florida!"

Kobee's Fun Facts

The average manatee is 10 feet long and weighs between 800 to 1,200 pounds!

Manatees are large, but have very little body fat to keep them warm.

Manatees look like a mix of a hippopotamus and a seal. But they're actually related to the elephant and the hyrax, which looks like a small gopher.

Ahead in the water, a hermit crab tossed sand like a tornado. We zoomed over it. The crab chased us so fast, its shell flew off. I stopped. The crab caught up.

"Thanks for stopping," crab said.

"What's wrong?" I asked.

"I got carried away from my South Carolina home and couldn't get back. Now I lost my shell and feel scared," said the crab.

Kobee's Fun Facts

Manatees use two flippers and their paddle-shaped tail for swimming, steering, and stopping in water. Each of their flippers has three to four fingernails. They can also use their flippers to move along the sand!

"Don't worry, believe in yourself," I replied. "Jump on. We'll find you a shell, and get you home."

"What's your name?" asked Tess.

"Pablo," he said.

His claws tickled me. We soared south.

"Wow … a rocket ride!" Pablo shouted.

Kobee's Fun Facts

Manatees have hair on their upper lips and lower lips, seen as bristles or whiskers. They also have small hair all over their body to help sense their environment. Manatees can sense anything that touches their hair.

I surfaced for air, diving down, then up. Repeating this again and again.

Millions of shells lay just ahead. Pablo was thrilled. He jumped off and zigzagged left and right. Suddenly I saw something **BIG** eying up Pablo. "Shark!" I shouted.

Kobee's Fun Facts

Like humans, manatees are mammals. They breathe air too. Their home is in water so they surface every three to five minutes to breathe. When manatees sleep, they surface every twenty minutes for air.

Manatees surface, dive, and float in water, because they have very long diaphragms and lungs. Their lungs hold huge amounts of air which helps control buoyancy.

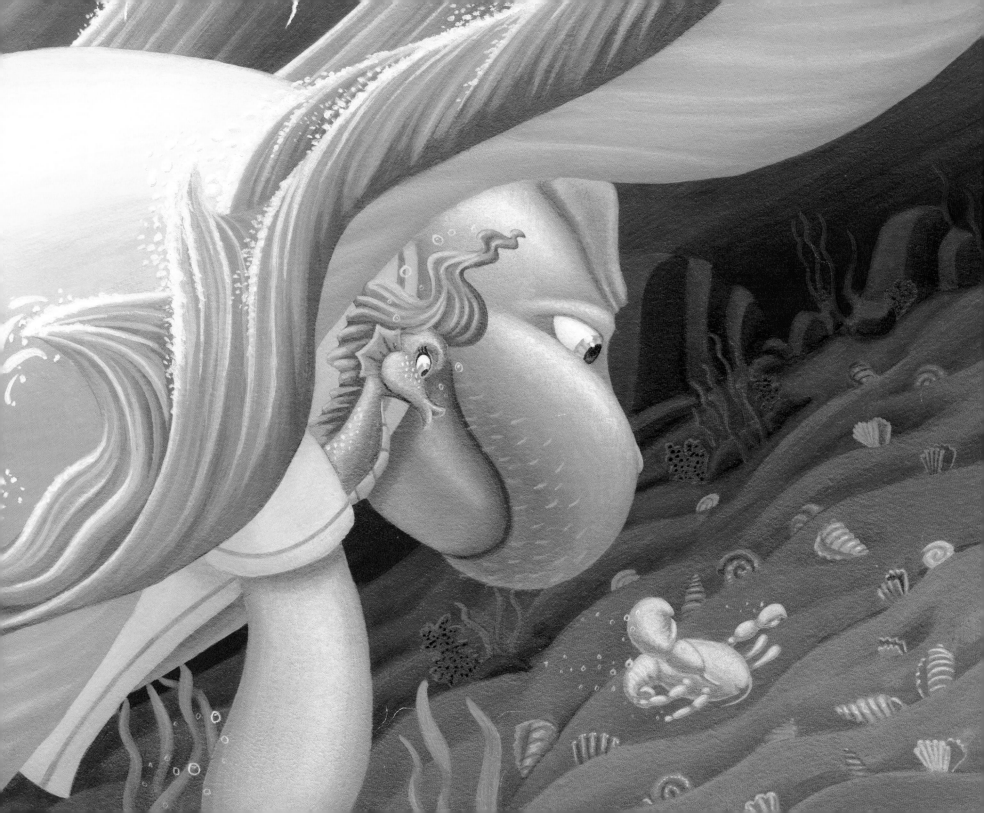

Kobee's Fun Facts

Manatees have no natural enemies. It's sad to say that their only enemy is humans. Watercraft can hurt or kill them.

Pablo looked up. The shark approached. Terrified, Pablo dug into the sand. Seconds seemed like hours. I raced over and rescued him. The shark turned and left. "All clear!" I said.

"Pablo ... you ok?" I asked.
"He's shaking," Tess said.
Then I felt him move.
"Thanks for saving me
Kobee," said Pablo.
"You're welcome," I replied.
I ate seagrass then sped south.

Kobee's Fun Facts

Manatees eat only plants, so they're herbivores. They'll eat ten to fifteen percent of their body weight in plants each day. That's about 200 heads of lettuce! Their favorite seagrasses include; turtle grass, manatee grass and shoal grass. They also eat water lettuce.

We passed the Chesapeake Bay Bridge. Suddenly, stunning shells dazzled us. "Pablo find yourself a beauty," I said.

He found the perfect one. Pablo proudly paraded around in his new home. Tess couldn't stop laughing.

Kobee's Fun Facts

Manatees don't have front teeth. They have "marching molars." When manatees eat tough plants with sand, their teeth fall out. Then their molars in the back march to the front. Manatees keep replacing their teeth!

Our journey continued. We whooshed into South Carolina.

"Pablo, you're home!" I shouted.

"No," Pablo replied. "You saved my life Kobee, plus I'm having fun! I'm staying with you guys."

"Fantastic," I said.

Tess cheered, "Yes!"

We swam lagoons loaded with seagrass. I ate another meal.

Kobee's Fun Facts

Manatees love shallow water because it's where plants flourish. They're found in coastal areas, shallow, slow-moving rivers, bays, estuaries, and canals.

Warmer water surrounded us. Florida
was close. Feeling thrilled, I belted out a,

"S-s-s-squeak!"

Tess and Pablo flew under my shirt.
"It's OK," I said. "I make that sound
when I'm happy." I felt them slip out.
"E-e-e-e-k," Pablo chanted as he
imitated me.
We laughed.

Kobee's Fun Facts

*Manatees talk to each other
with squeaks and chirps.*

"We're in Florida!" I shouted.

Pablo and Tess danced.

Soon we entered the St. Johns and went through Jacksonville. Then south to Blue Spring.

"What fun," Pablo shouted, clapping his claws.

But he lost his grip. He spun off like a spinning top!

"STOP!" Tess yelled.

I turned and searched everywhere – nothing.

Kobee's Fun Facts

Manatees love doing somersaults and swimming upside down!

Did you know that manatees can live to the age of sixty or longer?

Then two figures appeared. One was Pablo,
the other a giant sea turtle chasing him.

"Is Pablo OK?" Tess asked.

"No," I shouted. "That turtle eats crabs!"
I bolted between Pablo and the raging turtle. Its claws
scraped my tail. Pablo slid under my shirt.

"I almost went overboard!" Tess yelled.

"Kobee thanks for saving me ... again." said Pablo.

"Now hold on!" I shouted.

Kobee's Fun Facts

Manatees can only see the colors of blue and green. Their eyesight isn't their primary sense, especially in murky water. They are very tactile animals.

Kobee's Fun Facts

Manatees have two federal laws protecting them. They're the Marine Mammal Protection Act of 1972, and the Endangered Species Act of 1973. The U.S. Fish and Wildlife Service enforce these laws.

Seagrass was everywhere.

"Why do you keep eating?" Tess asked.

"Because I'm BIG, with no body fat." I said. "Eating keeps me warm."

Just then Pablo screamed, "Yikes Kobee, a BOAT!"

The boat whizzed over and just missed us!

"Whew ... that was close!" I shouted.

"Boats can't always see me," I said. "One of my manatee friends was badly hurt by a boat propeller."

"We're OK," said Tess.
Suddenly, the water turned warmer.
"We're in Blue Spring State Park!" I
shouted.
"Look … hundreds of your manatee
friends," Pablo said.

Kobee's Fun Facts

Seagrass provides food for seventy percent of all sea life including the manatee. Florida has about 2.7 million acres of seagrass. Unfortunately, seagrasses are decreasing worldwide due to human coastal activities. Florida's making progress in restoring its seagrass levels, but more work needs to be done.

They gathered around me. "It's great being back!" I said. I smiled, grabbed my guitar, and sang my manatee song.

Everyone shouted, "We love you Kobee!" "Cheers for manatees!"

Kobee's Fun Facts

In 1981, singer/songwriter Jimmy Buffett, and Florida's governor, Bob Graham formed the "Save the Manatee Club." The objective of this award-winning, non-profit club is the recovery and protection of manatees, and their aquatic environment throughout the world.
www.savethemanatee.org